This book belongs to

_____

Walt Disney® VOLUME 13
SEASONS AND HOLIDAYS

WALT DISNEY FUN-TO-LEARN LIBRARY

A BANTAM BOOK
TORONTO · NEW YORK · LONDON · SYDNEY · AUCKLAND

Seasons and Holidays   A Bantam Book/January 1983   All rights reserved. Copyright © 1983 by Walt Disney Productions. This book may not be reproduced, in whole or in part, by mimeograph or any other means.

ISBN 0-553-05517-8

Published simultaneously in the United States and Canada. Bantam Books are published by Bantam Books, Inc. Its trademark, consisting of the words "Bantam Books" and the portrayal of a rooster, is Registered in U.S. Patent and Trademark Office and in other countries. Marca Registrada. Bantam Books, Inc., 666 Fifth Avenue, New York, New York 10103. Printed in the United States of America   0 9 8 7

Classic® binding, R. R. Donnelley & Sons Company. U.S. Patent No. 4,408,780; Patented in Canada 1984; Patents in other countries issued or pending.

There are some days that you know are going to be special before you even get out of bed. "Today is different," you say to yourself. "It's a holiday and something wonderful is going to happen!"

But what is a holiday? It is a special day set aside for rest or play or for remembering something important or someone great.

Each season has its own holidays for us to look forward to. Every holiday has its own customs that make it special.

Join Mickey and his friends as they take you through a year filled with holidays we can all celebrate together. Have fun!

It's New Year's Eve and Mickey is having a party. Minnie, Morty, and Ferdie are helping Mickey get ready. Morty and Ferdie are very excited because this is one night that they are allowed to stay up late.

Morty is making funny paper hats for the guests to wear. Ferdie is cutting colored paper into tiny pieces for confetti. When the clock strikes midnight, they will throw the confetti into the air to welcome the New Year.

"Look at the clock," cries Mickey. "Let's get out the noisemakers!"

"Ten, nine, eight, seven, six, five, four, three, two, one," everyone counts backward together.

"The New Year is here!" Minnie announces.

"Happy New Year!" everybody cries.

On Saint Valentine's Day, it's fun to tell people how much we like them. This custom started a long time ago in Rome. The Roman people used to think that there was a god named Cupid, a chubby little fellow with wings.

According to the old Roman stories, Cupid would fly around shooting arrows into people's hearts. These arrows were soft, like magic feathers. They didn't hurt at all, but were they powerful! Anyone who was shot by Cupid would fall in love instantly.

Is that why Goofy is trying on those wings? Doesn't he look funny?

Watch out for Cupid, Mickey! Too late. That must be why Mickey is decorating his valentine with all those hearts.

But Mickey has signed it, Guess who? Do you think Minnie will be able to guess who sent it?

Can you think of a day on which sunshine brings bad luck?
Groundhog Day is the answer. On February 2, people watch their
favorite groundhog come out of its burrow.

If it is a cloudy day, the groundhog won't be able to see its
shadow. Great! That means spring will soon be here. But if it is a
sunny day, the groundhog will be so frightened by its shadow that it
will run right back into its burrow. That means six more weeks of
winter! Too bad, Goofy! You may have to wait a long time for that
fishing trip.

February is a month for special birthdays. Every year in February, we celebrate a holiday called Presidents' Day in honor of all our presidents.

On this day, we especially remember the birthdays of two of our favorite presidents—George Washington and Abraham Lincoln.

The weather is finally getting warmer. There are days when
you don't even need a coat. But the trees get new ones just
the same—in shades of green, yellow, pink, and white. Spring
is here.

Every spring, Grandma Duck invites Donald's nephews to
see the new baby animals on her farm and to help her plant her
garden.

This year the boys can't wait to get home to plant a garden of their own. First they turn over the earth to make the ground soft. Then they bury seeds in the dirt. Soon they will be picking their very first flowers and vegetables.

April Fool's Day is a day on which we love to play tricks on other people. One April Fool's Day, Morty and Ferdie played this little trick on Goofy....

Morty and Ferdie are having a great time decorating Easter eggs. Each egg is special—some have stripes, others have polka dots, one has zigzags, and another has stripes and dots on it.

The Easter Bunny came last night and left baskets full of chocolate bunnies and jellybeans. The Easter Bunny loves to hide eggs in secret places. Who found a funny surprise at the Easter egg hunt?

Watch out, Grandma! The blue jay thinks
that new Easter bonnet would make a great
place to lay her eggs.

It's Mother's Day. Huey, Dewey, and Louie are planning a surprise for Grandma Duck.

She's a wonderful grandma—and boy, can she cook! The boys have decided to give her car a good cleaning.

See how happy Grandma Duck looks! Her car hasn't been this clean since the last rainstorm. And as a reward, she's baked a special apple pie. Yum!

For Father's Day, Morty and Ferdie would like to show Mickey how much they love him. Mickey is their uncle, but he's just like a father to them. He takes them places, and he never really gets angry at them, even when they're a little naughty.

"You've made my day," says Mickey.
"I couldn't ask for nicer nephews!"

The summer sun is shining brightly as Donald makes breakfast for Huey, Dewey, and Louie.

"It's going to be a hot one!" says Donald. "How would you fellas like to go to the beach?"

"Yippee!" reply Huey, Dewey, and Louie. Why, they have their bathing suits on already! "Let's go!"

"Look at those waves!" cries Huey. "How far do you think this one will take us?"

After their swim, Donald helps the boys build a sand castle. They decorate it with beautiful shells.

"This is the best one we've ever made," says Dewey.

"I wish we could take it home with us," adds Louie.

"We'll have to settle for a picture," Donald answers. "But we'll come back soon and make another one."

The Fourth of July is a birthday that the whole country celebrates together. Why? Because it is the birthday of the United States of America.

Instead of presents, people make lovely floats to show off in a big parade. Instead of a cake and candles, fireworks light up the sky.

Every Fourth of July, Mickey has a barbecue. He invites all his friends over for a grand outdoor feast.

When it gets dark, everyone will go to the park to watch the fireworks from the top of a hill.

School has been out for less than a month. Mickey hears Morty say to Ferdie, "There's nothing to do around here!"

"Let's have a picnic," says Mickey. "We'll go to the lake and pack an extra-special lunch."

"This lunch is terrific," says Morty.
"The ants seem to think so, too," chuckles Ferdie.

"What do you want to do now, boys?"
"I want to take a boat ride and do
a little water-skiing," says Morty.

"We could play catch," says Ferdie.
"There's so much to do, Uncle Mickey!
Help us decide what to do first."

Labor Day marks the last long summer weekend before school starts. On this day, people celebrate work. They do this by not working at all.

On Labor Day, Mickey and his friends visit the county fair. At a county fair, you can see the biggest pumpkins, the reddest tomatoes, and the fattest pigs. You can even taste a delicious, prize-winning pie.

Donald's nephews love to go on rides and play the games. Sometimes they even win a prize. What a weekend of fun!

"Autumn leaves make a crunchy noise when you walk
on them, don't they, Uncle Donald?"
"Yes, Huey, but I think it's time we raked them up."
"Okay, Uncle Donald, let's get started. We'll be finished
in no time."

"So much for work," says Huey. "How about having some fun?"
"Don't worry, Uncle Donald. We'll clean them all up again."

It's pumpkin-picking time again, and Mickey and the gang are off to Grandma Duck's farm to pick out their pumpkins.

Grandma Duck has invited them all to go on an old-fashioned hayride. They'll sip cider, sing songs, and enjoy the crisp autumn air.

Long ago in England people
believed in ghosts, witches, elves, goblins,
and all kinds of spooky creatures. So they
dressed up in scary costumes to protect
themselves. After all, what ghost would
harm another ghost?

On Halloween we still dress up in
costumes. Why? Because it's so much fun!

Here come Morty, Ferdie, and Donald's nephews now. They want to see if they can scare Daisy.

"I've been waiting for you," says Daisy. "Can you come in to my Halloween party? We'll dunk for apples, eat some pumpkin bread, and then we'll all go trick-or-treating."

When the Pilgrims first came to America, they had nowhere to live and nowhere to buy food. So they had to build homes and grow food to eat. They were lucky that the friendly Indians helped them.

Imagine how happy the Pilgrims were to see their first crop of corn growing so high! They decided to celebrate with a big feast.

The Indians brought food and taught them how to pop corn. There was so much food, so much company, so much to be thankful for! This was the first Thanksgiving.

Many of the foods we serve today at Thanksgiving were eaten at that first Thanksgiving. Turkey, cranberries, squash, corn, pumpkins, pies—don't you love Thanksgiving?

The first snowflakes of winter have barely
covered the ground. But Morty and Ferdie can
hardly wait to try out their new sleds.
"Last one down is a rotten egg!" yells Ferdie.

Donald is having fun making snow sculptures. Won't Daisy
be surprised to see herself standing in Donald's front yard!

Huey, Dewey, and Louie are going north with their Uncle Donald for a winter vacation. Since it is good sugaring weather, everyone is going to make maple syrup.

First they gather sap from the trees. Then they boil the sap in kettles over a fire. Huey, Dewey, and Louie can hardly wait to pour the thick brown syrup over some snow for a delicious maple treat. Yum!

For Mickey, skiing is the best thing about winter. He is an expert skier and a very patient teacher. Soon Morty and Ferdie are skiing down the high mountain slopes with their Uncle Mickey.

Donald has helped Huey, Dewey, and Louie clear the snow off the frozen pond. Today is a perfect day for ice skating. Doesn't it look as if Pluto could use a few lessons?

There's a special feeling in the air. Sparkling decorations, candy canes, and the sounds of carolers and sleigh bells all tell us that Christmas is on its way.

Best of all, Santa is coming! He's worked all year to make toys for the boys and girls he loves to surprise. Now his sleigh is packed. In just a short time, he'll be flying from roof to roof!

Before Santa comes, there's so much to do! There are presents to wrap, cookies to bake, and the house to dress up in its Christmas colors.

"I'll put some holly over this window," says Huey.

"I'll hang the wreath on the front door," adds Dewey helpfully.

"Let's not forget to hang our stockings by the fireplace," Louie reminds them.

Did you ever wonder why we have a Christmas tree?

Long ago in Germany, people thought that evergreens were magical. When all the other trees withered in winter, the evergreens stayed green and fresh.

"If we bring these trees inside, maybe we can share in their good luck," the people said. And that's how the tradition began.

"I love the way Christmas trees smell," says Ferdie.

"And they're great fun to decorate, too," cries Morty.

Christmas is so special, you will want to share it with all your good friends. That is why all the gang has gathered around Mickey's tree to sing their favorite Christmas songs and to share in the warm feelings that Christmas brings.

Santa's Calendar

This is how Morty and Ferdie keep track of the days left until Christmas. You can, too. Just make your calendar at least ten days before Christmas Eve.

1. Draw Santa's face on a dinner-size paper plate. Add cotton for his beard and eyebrows.

2. Cut a red triangle for a hat. In the middle of the hat, cut two slits 1" long and 3/4" apart.

1 2 3 4 5 6 7 8 9 10

3. Cut a long strip of construction paper 12" long and 3/4" wide. Write the numbers 1 to 10 across it. Be sure the numbers are about as big and about as far apart as shown below.

1   2   3   4   5   6

4. Glue a cotton ball to the top of the hat. Then glue the hat to Santa's head.

1 2 3 4 5 6 7 8 9 10

5. Fit the strip of paper through one slit in the hat and out the other slit. Position the strip so that a number shows through like a "window" in the hat.

6. Ten days before Christmas Eve, make the number 10 show in the window. The next day, pull the strip so that the number 9 shows. Move the strip one number ahead for every day until it is Christmas Eve. Have a Merry Christmas!

1 2 3 4 5 6 7